The Three Billy Goats Gruff

retold by **Susan McCloskey**

illustrated by **Patricia Beling Murphy**

D1496001

GReaT SouRCe
EDUCATION GROUP
A Houghton Mifflin Company

Once upon a time
there were three Billy Goats.
The name of the goats was Gruff.

The goats were hungry.
They had to cross a bridge
to get grass to eat.

Little Billly Goat went first.
Trip-trap, trip-trap.

He met a troll.
"Hey," said the troll.
"I'm going to eat you up."

Middle Billy goat went next.
TRIP-TRAP, TRIP-TRAP.

He met the troll.
"Hey," said the troll.
"I'm going to eat you up."

"Wait for my big brother,"
said Middle Billy Goat.
"Eat him instead."

Big Billy Goat went last.
TRIP-TRAP, TRIP-TRAP.

Soon he met the troll.
"Hey," said the troll.
"I'm going to eat you up."

"OH, NO YOU'RE NOT," said Big Billy Goat.

It was a good idea to cross the bridge.
The grass was yummy!